This book belongs to

_____

_____

Library of Congress Cataloging-in-Publication Data Available

10   9   8   7   6   5   4   3   2   1

Published in 2003 by Sterling Publishing Co., Inc.
387 Park Avenue South
New York, NY 10016

First published in 2003 in Great Britain by

GULLANE™
CHILDREN'S BOOKS

Winchester House, 259-269 Old Marylebone Road,
London NW1 5XJ

Text and illustrations © Charles Fuge 2003

Distributed in Canada by Sterling Publishing
C/o Canadian Manda Group
One Atlantic Avenue, Suite 105
Toronto, Ontario, Canada M6K 3E7

Sterling ISBN 1-4027-0707-X

MY DAD!

Charles Fuge

Sterling Publishing Co., Inc.
New York

My dad is the
roughest, toughest,
biggest, strongest dad
in the whole jungle.

He's as strong . . .

. . . as an **elephant!**

He has more claws
than an **eagle!**

His teeth are sharper than an **alligator's!**

And he can roar
as loud as a **lion!**

And he's as . . .

. . . where did everybody go?

What's that noise . . .

. . . and who's that?